The Brave
Little Tailor

Illustrated by Pythia Ashton-Jewell

AWARD PUBLICATIONS LIMITED

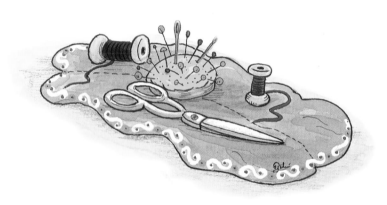

ISBN 0-86163-956-1

This edition copyright © 1998 Award Publications Limited

First published 1998 by Award Publications Limited,
27 Longford Street, London NW1 3DZ

Printed in Singapore

One summer's morning a tailor was sitting on his bench by the window, sewing away with all his might.

Presently, up the street came a peasant woman crying, "Good preserves for sale!"

This sounded very nice to the tailor. Putting his head out of the window, he called to the good woman.

He looked over her jars and jam-pots at length, and finally made his choice. The woman weighed out a half-pound for him, took her money, and went on.

"Now," exclaimed the tailor, "Heaven will send me a blessing on these preserves and give me added strength."

Taking the bread out of the

cupboard, he cut himself a slice and spread the jam upon it.

"This will taste by no means bad," he said, "but before I sup, I will finish sewing up this waistcoat."

So he laid the bread down near him and sewed away, making larger and larger stitches each time for joy.

Meanwhile, the smell of the preserves mounted to the ceiling where many flies were sitting, and enticed them down. Soon a swarm of them had settled on the bread.

The little man flew into a rage at seeing these unbidden guests! Snatching up a piece of cloth, he brought it down upon them unmercifully. When he raised it, no less than seven lay dead before him.

"What a brave fellow!" he said to himself. "The whole world shall hear of this."

In haste he cut and stitched a wide belt. He put on it in large letters: SEVEN AT ONE BLOW.

Then he bound the belt round his body and prepared to travel forth into the world.

From the cupboard he took a piece of cheese. Outside the door he saw a bird entangled in a bush, so he pocketed that too. Then he started on his journey.

At the top of a hill, he found a giant sitting beside some rocks.

"Good day, Comrade," said the

little tailor boldly. "I am on my way to see the wide world. Would you care to join me?"

"You miserable fellow, you vagabond!" said the giant.

"That may be," answered the tailor, "but here – you may read what sort of man I am."

He unbuttoned his coat to show his belt with the words SEVEN AT ONE BLOW upon it.

The giant read the words and formed a little respect for him. But, to test the tailor's strength, he picked up a stone and squeezed it until a few drops of water fell from it.

"Do that if you can!" said the giant.

The tailor dived into his pocket, took out the piece of cheese, and squeezed it until the whey ran out of it.

The giant could not believe his own eyes. Picking up another stone, he threw it so high that it could scarcely be seen.

"Well done," said the tailor, "but your stone must fall – and mine will not." Taking the bird from his pocket, he threw it in the air and it flew away.

"You throw well," admitted the giant, "but can you help me carry yonder tree?"

"Of course," replied the tailor. "You take the trunk, and I will carry the boughs, which are the heaviest."

The giant picked up the trunk, but the tailor, knowing the giant could not turn to see, jumped up into a branch. The giant staggered a short way with his burden, but soon he became tired.

When he called a halt, the wee tailor hopped to the ground and put his arms round the branches as if he had been carrying them all the while.

"You are too strong for me," said the giant, when he saw the tailor still fresh and vigorous. "Perhaps we had best go our separate ways."

The tailor agreed, and they parted.

The little tailor journeyed on until he became tired, and then he lay down upon the grass and went to sleep.

When he awoke, a messenger from the King and many other people were standing by him, looking at the words upon his belt.

"Ah," said they, "this must be a mighty hero and a great warrior!"

So, with much ceremony, the messenger conducted the tailor to the King, who was pleased to find such a useful man.

Promising the tailor a very fine house in which to dwell, the King requested of him his fighting services.

"Solely to serve you, Sire, did I come here," said the tailor, accepting at once.

The courtiers, however, became jealous and wanted to be rid of the tailor.

"If we go into battle with this man, and he strikes out seven at one blow, we shall not seem so brave," they said.

So they asked permission of the King to resign, saying they were not prepared to keep company with such a man.

The King did not wish to lose his old and faithful servants, but yet he feared the might of the tailor. For a long time he thought, and at last he sent for the little man to make him an offer.

"In the forest," said the King, "there live two evil giants who have created great havoc. If you will overcome both giants, I shall give you my only daughter in marriage and one half of my kingdom as well."

"Ah, that is something for such a man as I," thought the tailor. "A beautiful princess and half a kingdom are not offered to one every day."

So he accepted the plan.

The King sent one hundred knights to render assistance to

the tailor. But when they reached the edge of the forest, the tailor bade them wait.

"He who kills seven at one blow need not fear two," said he, and he sprang off into the woods alone.

After a while he came upon the two giants lying fast asleep under a tree, both of them snoring so loudly that the branches above them trembled.

The tailor filled both of his pockets with stones and clambered up the tree. Then he let fall one stone after the other on to the chest of one giant.

At last the giant awakened. Pushing his companion, he said, "Why are you beating me?"

"You are dreaming," replied the other one. "I did not hit you!"

They lay down again. Soon the tailor threw a larger stone down upon the second giant.

"What is that?" he exclaimed. "What are you punching me for?"

They wrangled over it for a few minutes, but both being tired, they again fell asleep.

Then the tailor took the remaining stones and threw them down with all his might at the sleeping giants.

"Aha!" roared the two giants. Springing up like madmen, they struck at each other.

Then they set to in such good earnest that they beat each other about until they fell upon the ground.

The tailor went back to the knights. "The deed is done," said he.

The knights could scarcely believe him until, riding into the forest, they found the giants lying still under the tree.

Now the tailor rode back in triumph and demanded his reward, but the King regretted the promise he had made and thought of a new scheme by which to get rid of the hero.

"Before you receive my daughter and half my kingdom," said the King, "you must perform one other deed. Out in the deepest woods there runs a unicorn. This animal does much damage, and it is up to you to catch him."

"I fear still less a unicorn than I do two giants. Seven at one blow, that is my motto," said the tailor.

Then he took with him a rope and an axe, and went away to the forest, bidding those ordered to accompany him to wait on the outskirts.

He had not to search very long, for soon the unicorn came rushing at him in a great rage.

"Softly, softly, that is not done so easily," said the tailor, springing behind a tree.

The unicorn, rushing at the tree, fixed his horn so fast into the trunk that he could not draw it out again.

The tailor tied the rope round the neck of the animal, and chopped off the horn.

Then he led the unicorn before the King. Not yet willing to give the reward, however, the King requested the capture of a wild boar which was a danger in the forest.

The tailor agreed and set out again.

When the boar saw the tailor, he ran at him. But the tailor sprang into a nearby chapel and out again at a window on the other side. As the boar ran in, the tailor closed the door from outside.

Thus the beast was caught, and the King was compelled at last to keep his promise.

The wedding was celebrated with much splendour, and the tailor became a prince.

One night the Princess heard her husband talking in his sleep, saying, "Boy, stitch up these trousers, or I will lay the yardstick over your ears!"

In the morning, she told her father she had discovered the Prince was only a tailor.

"This night," said the King, "leave the door open. When he is fast asleep, my servants shall enter, bind him, and carry him away."

The Princess agreed. But the King's armour-bearer, who had overheard all, went to the Prince and warned him.

That night, when the Princess believed her husband asleep, she arose, opened the door, and lay down again.

The tailor, however, was only feigning sleep, and said loudly, "Boy, stitch up these trousers quickly, or I will beat the yardstick about your ears! Seven have I killed with one blow, two giants have I overcome, a unicorn and wild boar have I caught – and shall I be afraid of those who stand outside my bedroom door?"

When the men heard his words, they ran away in great fear, and never again did any man in the kingdom dare oppose the brave little tailor.

Thus he became King, and so he remained. On his head he wore a golden crown studded with jewels, and on it were the words: SEVEN AT ONE BLOW.